Treat Us Generously

Treat Us Generously

જી

June Everett

RESOURCE *Publications* · Eugene, Oregon

TREAT US GENEROUSLY

Resource Publications
An Imprint of Wipf and Stock Publishers
199 W. 8th Ave., Suite 3
Eugene, OR 97401

www.wipfandstock.com

PAPERBACK ISBN: 978-1-5326-3129-0
HARDCOVER ISBN: 978-1-5326-3131-3
EBOOK ISBN: 978-1-5326-3130-6

Manufactured in the U.S.A.   SEPTEMBER 19, 2017

PART I

Chapter 1

ૐ

THE RADIO WAS SCRATCHY with the sounds of Glenn Miller. Static faded in and out as the rhythmic mellow sounds of his orchestra strained over the airwaves from WBZ Boston. The radio console, stood majestic in its place in the living room; while "In the Mood" blended with the laughter and talk of my uncles . . . the lusty sounds of my childhood.

Ella and Dorothy were probably there too, but I could not tell. But you could always tell the booming voices of Uncle Irving, and the smooth sound of Cary Grant, that is, my Uncle Lou.

They had long ago chased me upstairs, where I lay in my big bed in the large front bedroom. The railing that encircled the long upstairs hall just outside my bedroom door, made it easy for me to to be a part of almost everything that happened or was said in the living room below.

Yet, though our house always seemed very exuberant, it seemed to me that almost nothing happened in our town, except the War. That seemed everywhere, though it was supposed to be very far away. Everyone talked about it. Everyone lived it. Ration coupons . . . for groceries . . . traded, bought, stolen. No one had a new car; drove something they had for years, or something second-hand or nothing at all. Newspapers talked about some attack or plan. You couldn't ride the Digby Boat or take a train. Sometimes you would get down to the station, and the trip to Halifax would be a troop train and no one else was allowed on it, even with a ticket. I don't think people splurged at all. Not on food, or lights, or clothes, or things, or life.

And so on those summery nights, everyone sat on the big porch with the radio somewhere nearby. We had been in Bridgewater forever, but now, with the War, lots of new people kept moving in. Something to do with the CNR or the lumber mill down the road. And lots of women, too, working in the cotton mill, or that new plant, think it might have something to do with rubber, down the LaHave Highway, that the Navy or someone had just built.

Sometimes, my uncles and friends would go out to Ketepec for dances in the old Casino out there, and they would come back awfully late to our porch, and again, brought along Glenn Miller.

Our home was really a member of our family. An old, big, and even a gallant house with a large sweeping lawn out front and 3 garages out back. Through the Depression, I had heard it cost a lot to keep it going, and there was more than one cold room through those winters. But it was like our child too, and we managed it. And now, with the War, my grandmother decided to rent out the caretaker's place in the back-it was just a very large kitchen with 2 bedrooms. And she also rented the 3 back bedrooms upstairs, to girls who worked in the new spice plant opened by Batten's; or to young wives whose husbands were shipped overseas. One even brought a baby.

To me the best of the house in Bridgewater was the long driveway that wound in from Aberdeen Road. Aberdeen Road was really the highway, the busy road to Halifax, 60 miles away. On any day you could sit on that large front porch with its old uncomfortable chairs and couches from the family antique store-just old second hand stuff to me-and watch the traffic, rushing to the city. There always seemed to be lots and lots of cars and trucks, and even that new fangled station wagon, so sharp with its long shape and side wood paneling. It was a busy two lane road and I was really frightened to cross it by myself even to visit Isabelle, though my grandfather said just run across.

Mostly I liked to watch for Uncle Lou. He had a shiny convertible that he drove back and forth to Halifax a million times a week, and then afterwards was always washing and polishing it. My grandmother never saw the use for that car. It was cold in the winter even when the top worked. It had only two doors and hard to climb into or to somehow get out of. There really wasn't a trunk, because it had a rumble seat back there, which I loved, like I loved Uncle Lou.

I didn't know why that summer seemed so special to everyone. But probably because 'the Boys' were going away . . . to War. Uncle Lou was going up to Camp Borden in Ontario and the Air Force. And no one knew about Uncle Irving; he just wanted to join the Army, if they would take him on. He had an ear injury from a sledding accident way, way back, and he was looking around for some easy small town with a not too efficient recruiter.

Chapter 2

꒰ꕤ꒱

UNCLE LOU WAS TAKING his Chrysler convertible to New York before he lost any more freedom, he said. And Ella was not going as usual. Just him and Skip. Cary Grant and Clark Gable, taking that gorgeous car to New York City.

Up and down the rolling hills of Nova Scotia, and across bridges over rivers with fast currents, rushing toward the rough Bay of Fundy. The trip would take probably three days over a rural Maritime Province landscape and then Maine and the New England states.

The two-lane highway curved and wound through picturesque historical towns, surrounded by peaceful farm-lands and vivid forests, which hugged the rocky coast of the Atlantic Ocean. Old lighthouses could be seen from the many twists of the road, often placed on a coastal island seemingly sized just for it. But the Bay of Fundy was its own showcase, the highest tides in the world, and amazing falls which reversed direction at each change of its tide as it reached the port city of Saint John.

Saint John with its grand harbor. No matter how cold a Canadian winter, its waters never froze. So the big cargo ships of America or overseas were often docked at its piers. Sailors and Merchant Marine were a common sight, and yet that town was as blue as could be. That first evening in Saint John, the bootleggers seemed to almost hand out calling cards, and Lou and Skip soon found themselves in some well-known backshop off Main Street.

Lou met Marge that night. I don't know. I think a sister to one of the guys at that back room tavern. And Skip probably went his own quiet way. Just a smile; it was easy for him.

I was to grow to love Marge. She was warm and loving and stylish and girlish and real. But Uncle Lou was married to Ella, and though Marge followed him everywhere throughout the War, she never became my true aunt. A loss for all of us.

The day after; Maine. It really felt like southern Canada and they again rode through thick woods and terrifying curves on its coastal roads that would eventually take them through to Boston. Most folks didn't have cars or gas to travel long distances, so the guys moved quickly through the heart of the little highway towns, a yellow car with Nova Scotia plates almost shouting, we're going to the Big City.

Boston would have been just fine, but New York . . .

Chapter 3

NEITHER THE DISTANCE NOR the international border between St. Stephen and Calais (Canada and the US) made much difference to the guys. The first true excitement came in New York; the George Washington Bridge crossing. A magnificent structure that didn't linger on the Hudson River at all, but wanted to rush to the other side. The other side, Jersey.

Uncle Lou's 92 year old grandmother lived there and he had this overwhelming wish to see her. She didn't raise him. She just loved him. She was his undisputed champ. She lived a little too far away now, and she didn't travel too well of late. Perhaps it was his boyhood memories of visits to New York, parks and tall buildings, wild rides on subways, just the two at the zoo or museums, with a blend of thoughtful gestures and understanding words. And now her move to Jersey, to a nursing home, after an accomplished life in America, a successful home-a wife, a mother, a grandmother of a grown man (unusual for the times).

Mrs Kamarsky was tall . . . 5ft 7. And he, well over 6 foot, felt like a giant as he hugged her tightly. With pride, he introduced Skip.

"Well, young man," she looked at Lou, still a touch of a Lithuanian accent, never gone, through many years in the States. She had worked hard, from the moment she had arrived, to rid any disagreeable trace of the Old Country. She had gone to night school and learned to read, write and speak the new language. Learning bookkeeping, she had married Leonard, a photographer of local renown, and together they had prospered.

She had struggled to arrive in America, using Hilda Schmidt's borrowed papers by necessity. Traveling months, first by train, with many stops crossing unknown and unkind borders, then by wagon or even walking across half the continent to Rotterdam and a ship on which her cousin had purchased 2 important tickets. It was a harrowing cold winter trip across the Atlantic, but they had made it to New York and the home of Uncle Nathan, a sympathetic relative to her father, whom she had never met. She had escaped to a land without terrors; unlike the interminable troubles of tyrannical Russia, pograms, poverty, conscription, denial of education for women, for Jews, for the poor.

And then it was Europe who wanted our young men to go overseas to fight in their Great War. She hated the sound of the word, war; but now far away. And still, Leonard, American-born in this peaceful place on the still quiet side of the Atlantic, thought that he should go. She had escaped to a land without terrors, unlike the never forgotten ones of the past. She should be safe from the many dreaded hostile backward motions of War. Leonard didn't know Europe, was not frightened by strangers in uniforms with weapons. Had never seen cities and towns in foreign countries, with their very earth destroyed, and then left as someone else's pain.

He came home, even decorated, and to a glorious feeling of a proud America. The family now was filled with noisy children, even a dog, a business that grew, and no more fighting.

But there was to be unhappiness ahead. For Mrs Kamarsky, too many decades spent alone. Too many years without Leonard, and then a grown family scattered to all parts of a large country which promised many rainbows and much success. It was such memories, even so, that gave her that unconquerable vitality.

"I know you have to go," she half-whispered to the young Lou, named for his grandfather, "and you'll be so handsome in that uniform.

"But why the Air Force? Those things aren't safe!"

"Why do you say that, Bobby?" His name for his stately grandmother, who maybe cared a bit too much.

"I know," she almost whispered. "They burn and crash, and over the water too. I hear the news." Mrs Kamarsky always had her radio on, and worried over every item mentioned. But she was right about this one.

"You know I'll be fine, right Skip?" Lou said in a quiet prayer.

I hardly knew Skip at all. Just the snapshots that my brother, Geoffry, and I found in a trunk in the attic. Skip and Uncle Lou on the golf course. Skip, with the swing of a Hogan, a model of stance, in fashionable knickers, facing a perfectly groomed green ready to tee off down the fairway. And Uncle Lou, best friend, looking toward the faraway flag, quietly waiting his turn. Golf courses in Nova Scotia were restricted. The game, the course, for sure, must have been Skip's doing.

In New York, the game was baseball. It was a game of love in Nova Scotia, but not easy to see. Sure we all played, on sandlots, knew the major stars and their stats, bragged about favorite teams from large American cities where we quickly learned geography locations of states and distance from each other and us. The Nova Scotia favorite was the city closest to us, that is Boston and their Red Sox, only 400 miles away.

But to see ease and grace on a very green ballfield, the speed of a runner rushing between bases because of some wild pitch, the true blessings of talent, the strong blind faith of the fans, and the game itself, with your own eyes; that was still an improbability.

At home, you saw such paradise in newsreels. There were no broadcasts on our radio stations. You could not hear the crack of the bat, the excitement of the crowd, or even the bias of the home team announcer. The newspapers told you about those heroes, the big hitters, the rare feats of magnificent homers, so beautiful and certain, as they flew past the faraway fence. Every day, the Chronicle Herald would report on the games from nearby Boston or even faraway Chicago. Places I never expected to visit, but could pinpoint on any map, with batting averages included.

The New York Yankees were away that week in July. And that meant the Giants were at home in the old Polo Grounds, a stadium with impossible fences and very few home runs. But the Polo Grounds was the backdrop for Skip's first major league game. He thought it was a special place, but it was more than that. More than he ever envisioned. It was green. He could never have guessed that baseball thrived on the greenest of grass, unlike the barren sand of fields at home. It was beautiful! Men in full baseball uniforms right down to their cleats. Strikeouts, double plays, spectacular catches, speed goes with the runner. And the Giants won; beating St Louis.

Skip became dedicated to the Giants, right there and then, and so, he spent the entire week at the top of Manhattan, sometimes known as Coogan's Bluff, the Polo Grounds.

And Lou, he found Marge somehow, somewhere in that Big City.

Almost too soon, the little convertible, with reserved effort, made the trip home, and almost timelessly soon found itself parked on the long driveway in Bridgewater. In love with New York even more.

Chapter 4

THE AIR FORCE TOOK them both away. Camp Borden in Ontario. By train. Two thousand miles away. It makes no difference how you say it. Even a trip to a city like New York gives you no preparation. You're alone that first day. The best friend taken away to some far place that you hope is still on the same base. The meanest guy in the world sleeps in a bunk right next to you. Regrets already.

"Well, you old herring choker, your father's a fisherman!"

And then you knew that these big shot idiots from Ontario were the real hicks.

Ontario was really flat. No more the rolling hills of Nova Scotia with its sea, its beauty, a power not more than 45 miles from anyone, anywhere, in the province, and usually much closer; and Halifax, historic, proud, busy, now a worried port that enemy ships of war will find its huge harbor tightly rooted on the Atlantic coast.

Marge came. Something about a brother living in nearby Toronto; and, of course, she found work immediately at the Toronto General Hospital.

Time did not go swiftly at Camp Borden. And in fact, it was obvious almost from the beginning for Lou, he was not going to make it overseas. When he came home after the war, he never told one war story. He was tough, but not fighting tough. I know he hated the routine, the food, the boredom, the mischief, the orders, the menial jobs, the lack of women . . . except for Marge in Toronto.

Marge was full of life, with long straight silken hair, a whispery voice, and even a bit athletic, who could swim, and golf, and love.

And he was married. There was Ella back in Nova Scotia at her parents' dairy farm down the LaHave River. Ella had graduated from Dalhousie University as a teacher, and was working at a little school down the river. But not for long.

PART II

Chapter 5

OUR FAMILY, THE ANTIQUE dealers; very popular with American tourists and their love with the automobile, which took them all over their country and ours.

People now talked of times before the War, and after the War. But to me, it was 5 years ago and uniforms had long been put away.

Uncle Lou had divorced Ella, and as a surprise to everyone, he married Nancy, on a trip back to New York for a cousin's wedding. Marge had followed him back to Nova Scotia, but love, I guess, wasn't enough.

So Lou moved to New York, where I thought he truly belonged. Fast cars, sharp clothes, baseball and racetracks.

He brought Nancy to Nova Scotia for his honeymoon, and then each summer, would come back home to Bridgewater.

And so would I.

My father too had come back from the War, and we moved to Saint John, then a stretch of 300 miles. But there was no interfering with Bridgewater. It was home. A big house that rambled along, with a player piano in the front room, which played my favorite tunes just by pumping on its petals (though I really couldn't play a note). The rollers were in the cabinet in the hall, and every summer I looked for my favorite, "Poor Butterfly". Nothing had been touched during those away winter months. And, in fact, I felt like I had never been away. My favorite house was filled with fun, uncles and grandparents I adored.

Our family home, built in 1900, boasted of that old-fashioned gingerbread trim, a wraparound front porch, a kitchen with the latest appliances and stuff, including the town's first automatic Bendix washer, fireplaces with marble mantles in bedrooms and sitting rooms. But only one bathroom. Magnificent in style, with a fine marbletop sink, almost surround mirrors, the largest of tubs standing on its clogged feet, and a big sunny window overlooking tops of trees as they worked their way down the slope to a casual brook. And always a waiting line in the hall.

Chapter 6

I LOVED THE DRIVE along the country roads with Uncle Dave. The road to Lunenburg had invented twists. It was almost a scenic thrill ride with blind knolls that seemed to rush down into the river water before being caught by a quick, almost hidden hairpin turn at the very last minute. And then we'd bypass that town and go a little farther to Blue Rocks seeking a dry sink, which had been used vigorously only a couple of years before; before water and sewerage systems had been invented in the remote areas of the province.

The wood on it had the strong lines he admired, and even topped with inlay. It would be attractive to the tourists who would ooh and ahh over their find. It was quaint. Uncle Dave liked that old sink.

Tidy, thin, tall Margaret McLellan, her white hair pulled back in a bun, wore an apron that appeared handmade. As she greeted us, she quickly discarded it behind a kitchen door. I somehow didn't really think she was just a farmer's wife.

"This dry sink has been in our family a very long time, since my uncle brought it up here from Philadelphia."

"It's very good looking," Uncle Dave muttered. "What do you want for it?"

He glanced over the room as he regarded this prize. A farmhouse to him was usually filled with many wondrous items in which the owner rarely knew their worth; but did know how to haggle . . .

No one ever called us anything mean to our face. We were the Cohens, or the Jews, who bought up old furniture. That was our part in the community. We were pretty well off according to local standards, and we were very good looking, blondish and fair. None of us could look back very far at all. Not past my grandparents, and a faraway place which felt like millions of miles away, and millions of years. And in truth was the Russia of 50 years ago. Our privilege was due to my grandfather, who sneaked out of Czarist Russia at 14. Started as a peddler on the back roads of Nova Scotia and became the owner of the largest department store in the county. And the good looks, and the blond hair; G-d's choice.

"Oh, I don't know. I have no idea what it is worth."

I loved this dance. Uncle Dave always, always had the seller give his price first. It gave my uncle an idea of what the owner thought it was worth, and, as he said, it belonged to them . . . so let them value it.

I know my uncle already envisioned it in the back of his turquoise blue Dodge station wagon, and was thinking of a good spot for it . . . in the house . . . I was hoping for the sunporch.

I hated when they put nice things out back in the garages. They would be all squeezed in together, and then be covered by those old high-button shoes, or a bunch of odd silver spoons or once popular phonograph records.

I got a little thirsty while they were talking about it. A fellow named Lawrence, quite sweaty himself, just in from the fields, got water from the pump at the kitchen sink for us both.

"Sure going to miss that cabinet. It's been sitting in that corner long as I could remember."

Mrs. Margaret McLellan said nothing. Her look said her nephew never noticed it before, and all of a sudden, now.

Uncle Dave was certainly the most quiet of all my uncles, but he was satisfied. He and Lawrence put it in the back of the station wagon, and we were on our way.

Dave's war years were full of battles, though he never put on a uniform. They say he drank, ran around all night, gambled, traveled, made lots of money and lost lots of money. Though to the 11-year-old niece who was with him on every road in NS, he never said anything at all.

We drove into the yard in Bridgewater. It was a bit too quiet. My grandmother didn't come out to the car; didn't come to look over the sink; didn't come to ask questions, give instructions, barely said hello.

"Dave, we have to get the big room ready upstairs . . . Jill, Grandpa left the radio blaring? Please go turn it off."

I loved Grandpa's stories about when he was a boy, but he told them best at 10 in the morning with tea. And now he wanted to walk to the back kitchen. He never cared about any room in the rear of the house, and especially that dark room. The house had had this huge kitchen when they bought it, and as they added those gorgeous electric appliances, the new stove with its remarkable true calibrated oven, and the extraordinarily wondrous automatic Bendix washer, they simply remodeled away making the kitchen half its original size. What was left was hidden behind a wall, saved with no plan, but considered usable. It had the old sink, the old oil stove, the old wringer washer, a small window, and the door which opened to the backyard.

We sat at the small table. Grandpa was never serious or cross or worried with me. But tonight, it was a grandfather who was forced to make a decision to a problem that wasn't his and he didn't want.

"Jill, you better go upstairs and get your things. We painted the sitting room last winter, and you will be comfortable there. Even fun there."

It was the big room down the hall from the parlor. With a place like ours, loaded with furniture, I knew in 2 minutes they could make it into a bedroom, complete with a new bed and mattress, and an old-fashioned bureau.

"It's got one of those new-fangled clock and radio things."

I had wanted a clock radio, but I didn't want it now. I wanted to stay upstairs.

"But, it's downstairs." They knew I loved the big room upstairs. The master bedroom. The best room, with its wonderful large windows where you could see the hill wind its way down from our house and beyond, as it searched for the LaHave River at the end of Aberdeen Road. A very large room with even living room furniture nestled in front of a fireplace, I guess, for those chilly Canadian nights.

Neither grandparent wanted to climb stairs anymore, so they took the study, tucked away behind the dining room on the main floor; took out all those gorgeous bookshelves and made it into a bedroom with a huge closet.

Chapter 7

THE DOWNSTAIRS SITTING ROOM. My summer bedroom. One could even describe it as opulent. A large fireplace with a mantle of marble. My grandmother never lit any of the fireplaces in our house. She found no charm in their sound or light, even winter warmth. They reminded her of the old country; an essential there which was dependent on scarce wood, and too often dangerous.

There was a wonderful ceiling medallion which circled a brass light fixture. And even matching molding on the rise of the wall. And a huge heavy wooden door ensured quiet from the hall.

My upstairs room went to Skip. But why? What was he doing in our house, and why the best room in the house? What about a back bedroom?

The Boston Red Sox were the home team. Though 400 miles away, and in the States. But we were from the same roots, even before the American Revolution. Many of the Maritimers' ancestors were the United Empire Loyalists. Those who may have lost that war, that is the Revolutionary War, and made their way to Canada after the 1783 treaty. Still family. Lots of connections; relatives, culture, food, sport. We were really another piece of New England with a hidden geographic border.

Ballgames came in from the States on the Boston radio station WBZ. Nova Scotians tended to root for the Boston teams, no matter the sport, but there were still a few that rooted for other teams, like the Yankees. Or, in the case of my brother, the Washington Senators.

But Skip liked the New York Giants.

Of course, it was raining the day that Skip came. The taxicab dropped him at the end of the driveway, pulled in only slightly from the traffic rushing down Aberdeen Road. I was sitting on the sunporch by myself. My grandmother, who could hear a car door slam in the next town, moved me out of there. But I had seen a haggard thin man with shamefully skinny legs, dependent on a cane, carrying only a small brown leather valise.

The hall echoed with the voices.

"Did you have any trouble on the trip?"

Probably a nod, as he struggled through the hall, toward the wide staircase.

The War again.

The handsome Skip! The athletic Skip! The charming, cheerful, witty Skip!

In Burma! A prisoner of war! On a death march!

And he had made it home! To us! In Bridgewater!

Chapter 8

UNCLE LOU WAS LIVING in New York . . . He had become a true New Yorker to me. The New Yorkers all seemed to live in small apartments, and yet they were always bragging, and acted like they knew everything. And they never stopped telling you the price of everything they bought. 'I paid $25 for this shirt, $3000 for my brand new automatic Chrysler, and we ate at the Tavern on the Green, and the niece of Ethel Merman was at the party the other night,' and . . . well, you get the idea.

My uncles were away that afternoon. Uncle Dave, probably in Chester Basin or Mahone Bay. And Uncle Irving. I'm not really sure. He hadn't been home in a couple of days. Uncle Irving was nothing but fun. We liked, that is, he liked to go swimming. And he would close his shop a couple afternoons a week, and drive down the LaHave River, where he knew a spot that was truly his, a place a little away from the highway. Sometimes his pal would join us, but, mostly I sat on the bank while he swan across the river and back, and I tried to tan up a body much too blond for such ambition.

Or often at night, he would join his buddies at the local Legion Hall. My grandmother couldn't take this. He had won a scholarship to Dalhousie University, when that school rarely gave away the right time, and yet he had still wanted to join the Army. And did.

And now he just loved life with no orders.

My guess was that he got friendly with the cosmetic representative that stopped by Atkins Department Store that week. She had an exciting territory to us, Nova Scotia, and New England like Vermont and New Hampshire and Maine.

She was a bleached blond, not a common sight in our parts (that was only in the movies), before Clairol and California made it okay, and accepted . . . And she wore lots of makeup. I saw them walking along the riverbank by Uncle Irving's store, but my uncle saw me even faster.

"Jilly, don't say a word at the house."

Of course, he didn't have to tell me or attack me with the truth.

He often left the store, hardly locking its door, during a slow day. And there seemed to be a bunch. Went for a cup of coffee at the restaurant next door, or visited Roger, who owned Henderson's, the family shoe store across the street. But Roger had help and was continually busy. Satisfied with a few sales, Uncle Irving considered the flooring business 'hard work'.

I never knew how old my uncles were back then. Of course, they were probably quite young, maybe late 20's, or even 30, I imagine. In my eyes and even still, they were all knowing. They had been in the War. Five distant years ago.

So I said nothing.

And his Dodge stayed parked in our yard all that week.

So my quiet Uncle Dave opened the store every day, staying till 6, leaving the antiques and tourists of his business with my grandfather.

The cash register rang often, we made deliveries, he called Halifax for essential inventory, insisting on delivery now. He scrambled. He hustled. And the business might even have shown a profit. When Uncle Irving came back.

Chapter 9

$\mathcal{SO}$

SKIP LIVED IN OUR house that summer, in the master bedroom upstairs.

There were many joys in the Bridgewater house for
me. But probably the thing I loved the best was the beautiful piano, the player piano even, that stood proudly in the
corner to the right of the front windows. My mother and
my aunt learned to play on that piano, and, in fact, some
of their music, their favorite sheet music, was still in the
bench. My aunt eventually bought her own piano when she
had her own home. But we didn't. Maybe our house was too
small, or my mother cringed at the idea of piano lessons for
the children, an idea which she never enjoyed, or it was just
too expensive. Anyway, we didn't own a piano.

But I could walk into the big living room in Bridgewater anytime, and close the heavy oak doors, and just
pick out a few songs from that old sheet music left in the
bench. But best of all was the player part. Rollers were in
the closet under the stairs, and I would choose three or four
and play away many an afternoon. Over and over, I would
choose and sing to *Poor Butterfly*. The melody seemed dif-
ferent than those I usually heard on the radio, and told a

story I barely understood. But I could feel the anguish and poignancy and heartbreak in that music.

From somewhere, a tired voice came from a very thin and haggard man . . . over by the mantle, barely hanging on.

"The Giants are playing today, and I hear this radio usually brings in the New York station."

The American stations had the best programs. Stuff like "Father Knows Best", "Inner Sanctum", "Gunsmoke". Mostly it came from WBZ in Boston, seemingly coming up the North Atlantic to us in Nova Scotia. New York was much harder to bring in, but some of the radios in the house had that special talent, that is an aerial that could pick it up, particularly the big radio in the corner of the living room, which anyone hardly used anymore.

But the living room was mine in the afternoon! And, in truth, I never had an audience as I played and sang to my heart's content.

He turned the knob on that old radio. The scratchy sounds of long distance United States broadcasting came through. And then the catchy unfamiliar jingo, "Have a Knick, Have a Knick, a Knickerbocker Beer".

The Giants came up to bat. Their season, through half of July, was off to a sluggish start. But no matter for a certain nasty haggard old man.

More and more batters came running toward home plate ringing up the score beyond anyone's dream. And a very ordinary bruised man sitting by the radio quickly moved away. In his place was someone else; certainly a much younger man, full of excitement, listening to tales from the radio of Giant good fortune, led by the announcer's ravings of missed flies, of stolen bases, reluctant home runs, and then what grand fellows, Alvin Dark and even the rookie, Willie Mays, were. It was 1951 baseball. It was July, and the New York Giants, were playing at the Polo Grounds.

"Jilly." My grandmother.

"I'll be right back," I muttered as the radio shouted about a line drive.

"Jilly, Skip is sick. He shouldn't be downstairs at all. Go see if your Uncle Dave needs some help. He must have over 3 dozen high button shoes out there to unpack and set up."

Who cares about those old high button shoes. They were for the tourists.

The doorbell rang. No one ever did that. It was a very long and shrill ring. Trouble. Neighbors or friends usually knocked on the unlocked front door, or hollered yoohoo.

Really.

This was a stranger.

An impatient woman spoke directly to my grandmother. "Mrs. Cohen? I'm Skip's sister, Adrienne. I'd like to talk to him."

My grandmother suddenly grew nervous. And I knew it was not my place to say a word. But why not? He was just down the hall.

And the look from my grandmother told me to leave; right away.

There were secrets in my house now. And I was the one, and probably the only one, who didn't know them. So I went to help with the old high button shoes.

I just sat down on the stuffed rocker with the caned back.

"Why don't we take Skip for a ride when we go down the river?"

"We can't," my uncle answered. And we didn't the whole summer.

But Skip stayed in the game, that is, with the game. The Giants kept swinging, and Skip kept swinging too.

Chapter 10

TEA WAS THE ANSWER. A commitment to tea was a lifetime thing. Before it all, before Depression or War, there was tea.

Now my grandmother turned on her radio in the kitchen, and her favorite guests arrived. Folks supposed to be from a place in Middle America, but probably New York. Pepper Young, and Poppa David, and somebody Kramer. We were the only Jews in town, and there was very few us in the Maritimes. So I thought there were only a very few of us everywhere. I believed those Hollywood names like Tony Curtis. But those persons in the soap operas sounded like or acted like my relatives. I had never seen New York and had never seen a real actor-they all just lived in the States.

Sort of everyone had tea in late afternoon. They just seemed to drift to the kitchen.

My grandmother blended great tea, often with home-baked cookies, sometimes a favorite storebought. And even Hilda. Hilda, from the backcountry with that funny accent, and almost no teeth, was welcome at my grandmother's table at tea time. She came to the house around 8 every morning, and stayed there for my whole childhood. She was very kindly, but had a boatload of kids who caused her a gang of problems; drinking or wrecking that old family truck, or spending her welfare check somehow. The funny thing is that I never cared for Pepper Young's Family.

❦

The Giants seemed to play almost every day. But sometimes the static was unbearable and impossible. And Skip would get exasperated and frustrated.

"You know," he blurted one day, "during the War, I didn't see or hear baseball for years." Just the remember brought back the hurt on a once humiliated face.

"I thought I would never utter Burma again . . . to anyone . . . but it's here today. Even in the comfort of this room, on a perfect summer day like you can only find in Nova Scotia."

A perfect summer day; a shattered life.

The baseball game is ended. "But the Giants, they picked me this year, 'cause they are going to leave the rest of that league way behind."

You could hear the voice of the announcer trying to say something about that home run. But whose, we couldn't tell. Was there excitement in the announcer's voice, or despair? Was it the Giants or Dodgers?

Skip started moving out of the living room. The day had ended for him in faraway New York, but the real players were in Burma where the too thin frame had risked his life and survived, almost like those Giants, to play another day. Like a child, the covers of his bed could probably give him his needed sanctuary. He was struggling away.

It just came out. And I almost shouted, "We got Baxter's ice cream today." The best there was.

And for that moment, we were both children, and though we couldn't tell or rejoice in a Giants victory, he had chocolate and me vanilla, and we chuckled over some silly joke I had heard in school.

"You know, Jilly, I hear them riding you, 'cause they say you're too thin, and you eat like a bird and all and you're so small. But, don't worry, you are going to grow up to be a beautiful woman, with as many boyfriends as you'll want."

I don't know how he knew that I more than fretted about if the boys would like me, or I would find someone for skinny me.

"You'll have to choose. Oh, so carefully. The real secret, the real answer is trust. Not blindly, but wisely. Take your time; marriage is not the only answer. You won't be alone. You won't."

Okay. I thought. But I knew I would be thin all my life. I didn't know then, that thin was going to be so coveted, and, in fact,I was handed a gift. Parents wanted their children softig then, as it was really a feather in their caps, that they cared for their kids so well. Of course, those 'kids' were struggling with diets the rest of their chubby lives.

At the last bite of his cone, Skip walked toward the stairs. Not stumbling, this time. The Giants would play tomorrow.

Chapter 11

I WENT TO HALIFAX. My aunt always wanted me to come and visit her in the city. But why?

The magic of Bridgewater . . . 60 miles south . . . a pretty clean and predictable place, the beach by the highway, the rides down the river, the fun in the old garages, and surprisingly, Skip.

My aunt and uncle worked in the store they owned way down Barrington Street. So it was get up early and go with them, or sleep in and take the bus.

I had never been in a house by myself, not my own, my grandmother's, no one's.

So I eased myself into the kitchen, turned on "The Breakfast Club with Don McNeil" and squeezed a glass of orange juice in a somewhat new contraption.

Don McNeil and his gang in Chicago, marched around my breakfast table. It was fun, as they told their corny jokes, and interviewed some of the folks in the audience, and made me chuckle too.

They claimed it was only 8 o'clock in Chicago, two hours behind us. That city seemed both wonderful and strange to me, two baseball clubs and the Chicago

Blackhawks, tall buildings like New York, theater, a huge lake. Oh well, one day I'll see it.

The best part of the show was the singer, Johnny Desmond. A baritone, whose heart was heard with each song; yet he was still a big part of the fun of the show. And then this Italian fellow, I knew he was Italian, would sing "My Yiddishe Mama" . . .

> *"There's things I should be thankful for*
> *I've had a goodly share*
> *But as I sit here in the comfort of an easy chair*
> *My memory takes me slowly back*
> *To an Eastside tenement*
> *Three flights up from the river where my childhood days*
> *were spent*
> *It wasn't much like paradise*
> *Amid the gloom and all*
> *But there the sweetest lady*
> *One that I fondly call*
> *My Yiddishe Mama*
> *I miss her more than ever now*

The mystery to me was why that song hurt. My relatives, my Mom, my Grandmother, were all around me. I frankly didn't even understand tenement or river or gloom. And now, I have seen that glorious Chicago and I have seen more of the world, and Bridgewater is so very far away. And the song hurts still, more than I want it to.

I got dressed and went to the store.

Chapter 12

It was August. Even in a short summer season, August signals the beginning of the end of the lazy days with the comfortable summer weather of the Maritimes. Innovative August, knowing that fall could be minutes away, could be rainy or very hot or suddenly cool.

All week, I didn't hear about a home run, or a triple play, or a curve that outsmarted the batter. All week. My aunt and uncle didn't know a Giant from a Dodger, or even a Red Sox.

I guessed the Giants were managing without me. But not without Skip.

We dropped into Johnny Marshall's Antique Shop, just off Barrington. Auntie Ida had no intention of staying more than a minute and a half. I loved his stories, but to her, it was an Irishman and a beer and not always a quiet afternoon.

He had gained quite a bit of weight, since he was that callous rascal that drove around NS selling the Detroit Free Press, and a hundred items the farmers on the backroads never saw. And then he and Peggy came home to our Bridgewater, cozy in a back bedroom, though they said he spent the whole winter complaining about radiators that didn't really work very well and much more.

At five days old, when I first arrived home to Bridge-water, it was Johnny who picked me up at the front door, and he has never really let go. He used to come down all the time to see my uncles Dave and Irving, and I like to think even me. Though in recent years he became richer and lamer. That old rickety Ford was now a fancy Chrysler, and just couldn't make the trip to Bridgewater, hardly at all.

"Sit down, Blondie, and tell me about school. Are you still the prettiest and the smartest?"

Pretty! I looked funny now. My hair was far too curly, and would not go into a ponytail, the style of every teenage girl. But I was still a blonde; the blonde. There were really very few of us. Clairol had not arrived in homes yet. I was short and flat and disillusioned. Not the beauty everyone had prophesied. And some of the girls, like Marcia, were already really gorgeous.

Yet, I still led my class. Not the best idea in 1951, to be smarter than the boys. That summer, I decided, I would play dumb, like Marcia. And those boys could explain it all, everything, to me and then. . . . we'll see.

"Hear Skip is down in Bridgewater. That chap had some time in Burma. Beat him up forever. Not many survived those camps, those marches through swamps. And Skip, barely. Death marches they were called. Trying to stay ahead of us or the Japanese.

"His family doesn't want anything to do with him. Think he has some contagious thing from those jungles. Could be TB, just like they say for everything at Camp Hill Hospital. Even to blaming cigarettes; couldn't be those Canadian fags. Can you believe?

"Only your grandmother would take him in. She worried about you. But you look alright to me."

"C'mon, Jilly," Auntie Ida's shrill voice, "it's getting late and I got to get back to the store."

I knew Uncle Joe could manage. And I think Auntie Ida did too. But it was much more than a minute and a half. We got the bus back to the store.

Chapter 13

THE WEEK ENDED AT the Jacobsons' place at Black Point. It was hidden, way up a bumpy, curvy gravely road above the beach. . . . a typical chilly rocky Atlantic beach. But once you got up that rugged road, it was 3 attractive cottages around a big lawn filled with chairs and tables and chaises and a net for volley ball or badminton. And on Sundays, the relatives came. And talked, and talked, and ate, and ate, and talked.

There were really only a couple of cousins around my age, Pauline and Marian; the rest were older, and sort of stuck up, and no fun. I never admitted to being hungry there, as they served borscht and herring even lox, none it I wanted, at least for another 10 years, so Uncle Dave took me down to Hubbard's for my favorite, an egg sandwich and some pinball.

There was baseball on a distant radio when we came back. My uncles loved baseball . . . and the Giants were doing magic that August. They just kept winning . . . 16 games in a row, 37 of their last 44.

They won. Skip won. I just wanted to go home back to Bridgewater. And Uncle Dave wanted to get on the road before dark.

The house was awfully quiet when we got there. The family was pretty tired too. There was only minimum chatter and everyone seemed to scatter. I followed my grandmother to the kitchen, had a quick glass of milk, added a bit of chocolate, and went right to my lovely bed in my big room downstairs. Tomorrow would be another day.

Why were my dreams filled with swampy waters, body rashes, ragged clothes, marching and marching, no food, no sleeping, unbearable heat, men screaming, and men dying.

Why do people leave me . . . without saying goodbye. Why do they shout at me, and say they don't need me ever. Don't want me anymore. They can do it on their own. Why does it hurt me so inside, and still.

Chapter 14

THE DOOR WAS OPEN to Skip's room. It was as tidy as the morning I took my things and went downstairs. Both beds were made and the sun poured in from the big double windows.

A sadness crept into my being right away, and then emptiness, outrage, a feeling.

I just knew Skip hadn't moved downstairs.

"Where is Skip?" I asked, almost hollering as I ran down the steps.

"Sit down, Jilly, I have something to tell you about Skip", Grandma, all the love I would know for a lifetime came from her touch.

"I know he's gone. Don't tell me anymore. Why? Why did you wait till now?"

The kitchen just felt too tight. Way too small. And the lawn stretched forever and ever and ever. And I ran to the front, the tall trees, up the hill; cars streaming, rushing, crashing; Mrs. Harris' crowded corner store with everyone, everyone, wanting ice cream, especially little league teams laughing like in the midst of their baseball field.

Uncle Lou called that night and asked to speak to me. Though he thought he could make me feel better, his anguish became my anguish. His best friend was my best friend. Their sport, their game, was mine.

I now understood those old songs. *Yiddishe Momma, Poor Butterfly*. The words make no difference. It was their heart, maybe of a lost happiness, that gave them perennial life. And I learned about friendship that summer. It's not made of time of weeks or months or years, but rather the unrelenting rhythm of a lingering memory, a measure for a lifetime.

"Why did they send a man from Nova Scotia, which has barely six weeks of summer, to the cruel jungles of Asia?" my uncle asked. The rules of War.

And I learned about Skip, through the team he loved. For where does a team gain strength through a grueling, almost impossible season. A season that would not end, could not end, until it reached its triumph.

Chapter 15

THE SUMMER WAS OVER. I packed up shorts, tops, and a bathing suit well worn in Nova Scotia, in the waves of the cold Atlantic. I was going home by the Digby Boat, the Princess Helene. A ship, actually, with bursars, state rooms, restaurants, decks that circled the boat where everywhere was a great view, a gift shop. But for me, a four hour ride over what may be a calm or treacherous Bay of Fundy. My grandparents and uncles would drive me down to the harbor town of Digby, and for the first time, I would take the ride on my own. Did I look grown-up now, or just feel it?

School seemed to start almost the moment I got off that boat. And fall was the best; the promise of the Maritimes. The leaves had changed into Canada's favorite colors of autumn, shades of red and gold, a touch of orange, a dash of brown, governed by a protected chill in the fall air.

But they were still playing baseball in New York City. They, the Dodgers and the Giants.

Probably I should have listened harder. Should have known the players better, not just . . . Should have watched the standings change and change in that month of August. Should have sat down and rooted and yelled and even screamed with Skip, for Skip.

The bus dropped me off. When I opened my front door and looked at my father, I knew there was a kind of drama at the Polo Grounds that day. No static on the radio at all.

For this was the 3rd day of October, the true last day of summer, 1951. It was a tied series at the very end of the season. And probably a Dodger win. The ninth inning. The bottom of the ninth inning. . . . 2 men out and 2 strikes.

And then, then, a crack of the bat. A mighty crack of the bat.

The home run. The Bobby Thomson home run.

Heard in the Polo Grounds. In Brooklyn. And in Bridgewater. Everywhere.

The season was over. Long ago. Yesterday.

The Giants had won the game.

The Giants had won the pennant.

And it was Skip, once again handsome and tall and strong, who swept round the bases to home.

June Everett
May 2017

i Yellen, My Yiddishe Mama
_____

_____

_____

_____